R DARK yder

a novel

by

LIZ BROWN

H·I·P Books

Library and Archives Canada Cataloguing in Publication

Brown, Liz, 1981–
    Dark Ryder / Liz Brown.

(New Series Canada)
ISBN 1-897039-02-6

1. Horses--Juvenile fiction. I. Title. II. Series.

PS8603.R685D37 2004   jC813'.6   C2004-903729-3

General editor: Paul Kropp
Text design: Laura Brady
Illustrations redrawn by: Matt Melanson
Cover design: Robert Corrigan

  2 3 4 5 6 7   14 13 12 11 10

Printed and bound in Canada by Webcom

Kate Hanson finally gets the horse of her dreams, but Dark Ryder comes with a catch. Kate has just three months to turn him into a winner, or she'll lose her horse forever.

CHAPTER 1

Major Mack and Me

I opened the heavy wooden door to the stable. Inside, it was dark except for where cracks in the wood walls let in the morning sun. The warm summer air smelled of horses and hay. I loved that smell and the morning quiet, almost as much as I loved our old horse, Major Mack.

"C'mon, Major Mack, time for the morning ride."

Major Mack stomped his hooves and tried to

rub his head against me. Then he whinnied, almost like he didn't want to go.

"No more of that, old guy. The exercise will do you good."

I fed Major Mack some hay and then brushed his coat until it shone. Then I grabbed his saddle and bridle and put them on, tightening the leather straps just right. But as I walked Major Mack out of the barn, I noticed he was limping.

"Oh no, not again," I groaned. Major Mack often had a sore leg, but today it seemed worse than usual. My gramps said it was just old age: "Heck, even I limp sometimes," he always told me.

Much as I loved old Major Mack, it made me sad to see how much pain he was in. I had learned to ride on this horse, learned to jump with him, even done a few shows. We weren't good enough to win, but I still loved him. Maybe I loved him all the more because he was always willing to try so hard.

"Well, old boy, I guess we're not going for a ride today," I told Major Mack as I walked him back to the barn. "You take it easy and I'll see what I can do about that leg."

I took off his saddle and made sure that he had enough hay and water. Then I headed over the fence and across the pasture to Mr. Peterson's farm.

The Peterson farm was the largest horse farm anywhere around here. It had a stable big enough to hold twenty horses and a tack room that was nicer than my living room. Mr. Peterson was a big-city lawyer with piles of money. He'd bought himself a little place in the country, and now lived here most of the time. Horses were his hobby, and he had enough money to buy the best of everything.

"Hey, Pat," I shouted as I walked up to the stable.

"Hey, yourself," he replied. Pat was Mr. Peterson's groom. He was sweeping the stable floor as I walked up.

Pat was blond, tall and had muscles all over, like Matt Damon all buffed up. He was eighteen, just three years older than I was, but he acted as if he was twice my age.

Of course, I still look like a kid. I'm skinny as a rail, with a nose that's too big and hair that's never known a good hair day. No wonder Pat didn't really look twice at me.

But Pat knew horses. If anyone could help with Major Mack, it would be Pat.

"Got a problem," I told him, just a little out of breath from my hike. "Major Mack's leg is sore and swollen up."

"That's easy to fix," Pat replied, putting down the broom. "Get yourself a new horse."

"Pa-at!" I groaned. Even if Pat didn't really look at me twice, he still liked to tease me.

"Just an idea," he replied, grinning at me. "I told you last year not to take Major Mack out jumping, but did you listen? No. Now your poor horse is so old and lame, he can't even ride through the pasture. It's just old age, Kate."

"Yeah, yeah," I groaned. He was starting to sound like my gramps.

"Okay, end of the lecture. Here, I'll give you some stuff for the swelling. It's called a poultice. Just pour some in a bandage and wrap it around his leg. And call Doc Vickers if it doesn't get better in a day or two." Pat went into the stable and began to pour some medicine into a bottle.

I stood around waiting, then looked out at the training ring. There he was – the most beautiful horse I'd ever seen – Dark Ryder.

"How's that new horse coming along?" I asked Pat.

"I think Dark Ryder needs a shrink, or else a trip to the glue factory," Pat snapped back.

"Pa-at," I said, repeating myself.

"The only good thing I can say is that his rider got the horse she deserves. Mean deserves mean, if you know what I mean," Pat said, winking at me.

I had to laugh at that one because Pat was so, so right.

Mounted on top of Dark Ryder was his rider, Victoria Peterson. She was my age, the youngest of Mr. Peterson's kids and the snottiest. It wasn't enough that her dad was rich and bought her anything she wanted. Victoria was the kind of girl who had to remind you how rich she was. That's why Pat and I call her "the Princess" behind her back.

Victoria only came to the farm on the odd weekend during the school year – but now she was here all summer. Gramps asked why I didn't go riding with her. I just laughed. The Princess wouldn't be seen anywhere near me and Major Mack. Her nose was too stuck up to even look down at us.

I turned back and was watching Pat when I heard a loud CRACK from the training ring. Then I saw it with my own eyes – Victoria was whipping Dark Ryder as hard as she could.

I stormed out of the stable and shouted at her: "What are you doing?"

"None of your business," Victoria shot back.

She kept whipping Dark Ryder, trying to make him walk forward. But it was obvious the poor horse was afraid of something. He was shying away from a spot on the ground.

So I stuck my nose in again, whether it was my business or not. I walked over to where Victoria was riding and looked up at her sitting on the back of Dark Ryder. "Your horse looks scared, Victoria. Maybe you should *talk* to him before you start using a whip."

Victoria just sneered at me. "Look, I don't need advice from some stupid farm girl. I'm going to train this horse *my* way. Why don't you go home and go ride your donkey?"

She gave Dark Ryder one more snap of her whip. Then she pulled his head sideways and came right at me. I had to move fast or Victoria and her horse would have ridden right over me.

CHAPTER 2

A Donkey and a Whip

I guess what happened showed on my face.

"What's wrong?" asked Gramps as soon as I came into the house.

"Nothing," I said quickly.

"Come on, Kate, I always know when something's wrong with you. You can't hide it," he said as he dug into his lunch.

I guess my gramps is right about that. Ever since my parents died in a car crash six years ago, Gramps has been looking after me. The kids at school say that he's better than a real parent, and maybe they're right.

"It's just Victoria. She was making fun of me and Major Mack," I said.

"So you were over at Peterson's farm again today?" he said with a wink. "Daydreaming about all those pricey horses, too, I bet. Or did you go over to see that boyfriend of yours, what's-his-name?"

"Wrong, wrong and wrong," I said. "I only went to get medicine for Major Mack's leg. I was *not* dreaming about any of those pricey horses. And Pat is *not* my boyfriend."

"Whoa, little Kate, I was just making a joke," he said. "Sometimes you and your temper remind me of your mother."

"Sorry, I think I'm in a cruddy mood," I sighed.

"But I'm glad you're looking after Major Mack. That horse and me, we go back a ways, you know."

Yes, I knew. I had heard tons of stories about how Gramps and Major Mack used to win all the ribbons at the county shows. But now they were both old. My gramps was too poor even to have a vet look over Major Mack.

"So what did Victoria call Major Mack?" he asked.

"A donkey," I mumbled back.

"Well, Kate, now I know why you're mad. I've got half a mind to go over and talk to old man Peterson about the mouth on that girl."

"Forget it, Gramps. It's not that important," I said, feeling even worse now.

Gramps leaned back in his chair and sighed, "Kate, you know that if I could afford it, I would buy you the best horse in the world. Maybe in a few years if the crop prices get better. And if you save some of your own money –"

"I know, Gramps," I said. But in my mind I was thinking, *and maybe some day pigs will fly.*

*   *   *

The next day, the phone rang just as I was finishing breakfast.

"Hello?" I said, my mouth full of toast.

"Hey, Kate." It was Pat. "You left pretty quick

yesterday, so I just wanted to make sure everything was all right. And I was kind of wondering how the medicine worked with Major Mack."

"His leg looked a little better this morning," I told him. "Maybe you should become a vet."

"Nah, you need too much school for that," Pat replied. "And I wasn't real good at school. Anyhow, I was thinking maybe you should stop by later. I bet I can get you a ride on one of the young horses while Major Mack heals up."

My heart skipped a beat. Not only was Pat asking *me* to come see him, but I was going to get to ride one of Mr. Peterson's horses. *Way to go, Kate*, I said to myself.

"That would be great," I replied, almost choking on my toast. "How about I come over after lunch?"

"After lunch then. It's a date," Pat said with a laugh.

The minutes seemed to drag on forever. I tried to pass them by keeping myself busy. I brushed and patted Major Mack. I reread part of *Black Beauty*, my favourite book. I even put on a little makeup – not much because Gramps gets upset, but a little.

After lunch, I grabbed my riding helmet and ran over to Mr. Peterson's farm.

When I got there, I could see that Mr. Peterson was standing in the middle of the ring. Victoria was riding Dark Ryder around him in circles. "Great …" I muttered under my breath. Victoria was the one person who could spoil this day.

I walked straight to the stable to find Pat. He was doing some kind of work on the saddles.

"Hey, Pat," I said, grinning my very biggest grin.

"Hey, yourself," he said as I came through the door. "You ready to ride?"

"Yeah, but I think the ring is being used. It looks like Victoria is having a lesson with her dad," I said.

"I figured they'd be gone by now, but we might as well go watch them," Pat said. "Maybe you'll learn something from the Princess. I think she's taken some kind of course in advanced whipping and cursing. Probably got an A, too."

When we got to the ring, Pat and I climbed the three-board fence and sat on the top rail. Mr. Peterson was trying his best to help Victoria with her riding. As usual, Victoria didn't seem to be listening.

"Keep your eyes looking ahead and your chin up," Mr. Peterson called to her.

But Victoria was too busy looking at us to see if we were watching her. *What a show-off,* I thought to myself. *She's probably got a crush on Pat, as if somebody like him could ever be interested in a snot like her.*

"Okay, try this little jump," Mr. Peterson told Victoria. He pointed to a small fence in the centre of the ring.

Still staring at us, Victoria steered Dark Ryder towards the jump. The horse began to pick up speed, but Victoria didn't seem to notice. All she really cared about was putting on a show for Pat and me. Dark Ryder was barely three steps away from the jump, but still Victoria had her eyes on us. Talk about stupid!

Suddenly Dark Ryder stepped to the side, missing the jump completely. The quick movement made Victoria lose her balance. For a few seconds, she bounced back and forth on the saddle, leaning one way and then the other. Finally, she had to grab onto Dark Ryder's neck to stop herself from falling off.

"Stupid horse!" Victoria yelled. She took her whip and started hitting Dark Ryder on his flanks.

"Victoria, stop that," her father ordered. "It's not the fault of the horse. You weren't looking ahead like I told you."

Victoria just ignored him. She gave Dark Ryder

one final flick of the whip, then yelled over to us, "Pat, take this good-for-nothing horse back to the stable – or the glue factory." With that Victoria jumped off Dark Ryder and stomped off to the house. Her dad was left with us, shaking his head.

"If I had a horse like Dark Ryder, I wouldn't treat him like that," I said.

Mr. Peterson looked up, as if he had just noticed I was there.

"You think you can handle this wild one?" he asked me.

I nodded, shaking just a little in my excitement.

"Then give him a ride, Kate," said Mr. Peterson, turning to look at Dark Ryder. "No sense sending this guy back to the stable when he's all ready to go."

CHAPTER 3

Keep Dreaming, Kate

"Better go grab your helmet," said Pat. He held onto Dark Ryder's reins while I picked up my helmet from a fence post and put it on.

As I fastened the chin strap, I could feel my hands shake. I had never ridden a horse as big and powerful as Dark Ryder. This wouldn't be like going around the paddock with Major Mack. This would be *real* riding.

Pat led Dark Ryder over to where I waited and

handed me the reins. I put my foot in the stirrup and lifted myself into the saddle. I squeezed my legs against his side and whispered to Dark Ryder to walk. As he walked, I could feel his powerful muscles moving underneath me.

Slowly I moved around the ring, building up speed and courage at the same time. I tried to keep good form, good posture, the way real riders do at shows. I wanted Mr. Peterson and Pat to see that I could handle a horse like this.

But they weren't paying much attention. After a few turns around the ring, Mr. Peterson said it was time to take Dark Ryder inside.

I was a little sad to have to get off the big horse, but I knew he wasn't mine. I did my dismount, then gave Dark Ryder a hug.

"You're wonderful!" I whispered to him.

Dark Ryder shook his head as if he understood. Or maybe it was just my dreaming, but I swear that the big horse knew how I felt.

As Pat led him back to the stable, I got an idea. If my gramps couldn't afford a new horse, maybe he could afford to pay for lessons from Mr. Peterson.

That way I'd still get to ride a horse like Dark Ryder without having to buy him. It was a long shot, but it was worth trying. After all, I would have given anything to ride a horse like that again.

When I came home for dinner, my gramps was in the kitchen. "Hey, Gramps," I said cheerfully as I came in, slamming the porch door.

"Hey, honey. Looks like you had a better day today," my gramps said. "Were you visiting what's-his-name?"

"Gra-amps," I said. But it didn't really bother

me too much this time. Besides, I had to figure out how to ask Gramps for lessons. "Mr. Peterson let me ride Victoria's new horse, Dark Ryder."

"Well that must have been quite the ride," he said, chuckling. "I hear Victoria's horse is as ill-tempered as she is."

I just sighed. It seemed no matter how excited I got, my gramps still joked all the time. Right now I needed him to be serious.

"Gramps?" I started slowly.

"What's on your mind, Kate?" he said, turning to look at me. "I can always tell when the little wheels in your brain have come up with something."

"Is there any way I might be able to take riding lessons at Mr. Peterson's farm?" I asked. I crossed my fingers behind my back for luck.

My gramps set down the spoon he was using to stir the soup. "What's wrong with riding Major Mack around the farm?" he asked.

I was ready for that question. "Nothing," I started, choosing my words carefully. "It's just that I'd really like to learn how to jump, the way you and Major Mack used to," I paused and looked my

gramps right in the eye. "But Major Mack is too old to jump anymore, so I thought if I could take some lessons –"

From the look on Gramp's face, I knew what the answer was going to be. "I'm sorry, honey, but we just don't have the money this year. There hasn't been much rain and the crops don't look like they're going to come in that well."

I shouldn't have been surprised. The newspaper had been full of articles about the lousy weather. We'd had a too-dry spring and the forecast was for a too-wet summer. The harvest wasn't looking good.

"If this weather keeps up," Gramps went on, "I don't even know if I can keep the farm going. Riding lessons are just … well, keep dreaming, Kate."

But dreaming wouldn't give us what we needed. It took me while, but then I got another idea for making some money – and for getting the lessons I wanted.

CHAPTER 4

Deal of the Century

The next day, I woke up extra early. I tiptoed downstairs to our old computer and turned it on. My plan was to get Mr. Peterson to give me a job, but I knew I would have to impress him. So here I was, trying to type up a resumé to show him how much I knew about horses.

As soon as my resumé came off the printer, I grabbed it and raced over to Mr. Peterson's farm.

When I got there, I could see Victoria trotting

Dark Ryder around the field. Mr. Peterson and old Doc Vickers, the vet, were watching her. There was another man with them, an old guy chewing on a piece of grass. The three men were all talking to each other. All I could do was sit next to the barn and wait for a chance to speak to Mr. Peterson.

I had just stretched out my legs, when I heard a voice behind me. "Hey, Kate, what are you doing over here so early?"

"Hey, yourself," I replied, smiling at Pat. "I came over to talk to Mr. Peterson about something."

"Well, you're going to have a long wait. Mr. Peterson is busy trying to tell Doc Vickers that the Princess is a great rider." Pat rolled his eyes. "He even brought in old Bart Myers to watch the kid ride."

"Bart Myers?" I asked.

"Yeah, he's just about the best riding coach there is, at least around here."

We both looked over to the field where Victoria was riding. The ring was full of jump fences that were taller than me. Victoria was having a hard time riding around them.

"Those jumps are HUGE," I said to Pat.

"Yeah, they're from last night. Mr. Peterson invited some of the really good riders out to the farm. Don't worry, the Princess isn't stupid. She won't be trying those any time soon," he said.

But as soon as the words were out of his mouth, I could see Victoria steering Dark Ryder towards the biggest jump in the ring. I grabbed Pat's arm and pointed towards the two of them. "Looks like you're wrong," I said.

We looked over to see if Mr. Peterson noticed what was going on, but he was too busy talking to the other men. Just beyond them, in the ring, Victoria took her whip and gave Dark Ryder a smack. That made him go faster towards the jump. We held our breath as the horse got closer and closer to the huge fence. Dark Ryder had shied away from a smaller jump just yesterday. But this time the horse, like his rider, seemed more determined.

Dark Ryder pricked his ears forward. He built up speed rushing up to the fence, then took a powerful leap. He looked beautiful as he sailed over the fence – a perfect jump.

But Victoria wasn't ready for a jump that high. As Dark Ryder went up, she lost her footing in the saddle. The force from the jump sent her flying into the air.

Now all five of us were watching in horror as Victoria flew off the horse. This was the kind of accident where a rider could get badly hurt, or even killed.

"Vic –" Mr. Peterson cried out. He didn't even have time to finish her name.

Victoria came down and hit the ground with a thud. For a second there was deadly silence. We all began climbing over the fence to get to her.

And then she started crying. It was a terrible wail, full of pain and anger. But that was a good sign. If Victoria could cry, at least she hadn't broken her spine.

"Vicky, Vicky," cried Mr. Peterson.

"Don't move her," ordered Dr. Vickers.

The four of us bent over Victoria's shaking, crying body. No one knew how badly hurt she really was. Doc Vickers talked about calling for an ambulance. The other old guy just shook his head.

But suddenly, Victoria rolled over and blinked away her tears.

"Oh shut up, all of you," she said.

"Vicky, you're all right!" exclaimed Mr. Peterson.

As the men crowded around, Pat gave me a look. "I guess the Princess isn't all that hurt," he whispered.

"Guess not," I whispered back.

Out at the edge of the ring, Dark Ryder was still frightened and racing around. Pat and I walked towards him slowly.

"Here, boy," I called quietly. "It's all okay. It wasn't your fault, big guy."

Pretty soon Dark Ryder calmed down and we were able to grab his reins. Pat and I led him over to where Victoria had fallen.

Victoria looked up when we arrived with Dark Ryder. Her face was smudged with tears and dirt. She was holding her wrist, which looked like it was swelling. "Get that horse out of here. I never want to see him again!" she screamed at her father.

Pat and I looked at each other. Then I turned around and led Dark Ryder back to the stable.

I was brushing off Dark Ryder when Victoria stomped into the barn. She was followed by Mr. Peterson and Doc Vickers.

"Well, I don't know what I'm going to do with this horse," I could hear Mr. Peterson saying to Doc Vickers.

"Daddy, I'm *supposed* to be showing at the Royal Winter Fair this year," Victoria said. "I can't do it with that … that thing," she said, sneering at Dark Ryder. "He's out of control. He could have killed me today."

Victoria was making me mad. There was nothing wrong with the way Dark Ryder took that jump. The only problem was his rider, a girl who didn't know her own limits. But I bit my lip to keep from saying anything. I just started brushing Dark Ryder a little bit harder.

"I know how you feel, honey," Mr. Peterson said. He talked to Victoria as if she were a five-year-old. "Dark Ryder really is a mean and nasty horse. Maybe we should just have him put down," said Mr. Peterson. "What do you think, Doc?" Mr. Peterson was glaring at the horse.

No! I could feel my heart pounding harder. I knew I had to do something.

"Well, maybe –" Dr. Vickers began, but then I spoke up.

"No, you can't!" I said. Everyone turned to look at me. Pat was shaking his head, telling me to be quiet, but it was too late. "I'll buy him!" I blurted out before I even thought about what I was saying.

The whole group looked at me. They must have thought I had lost my mind.

"But you don't have any money, Kate," Victoria snapped at me. "I mean, you and your gramps are just a cut up from trailer trash."

That was even too nasty for her father. "Victoria, please," he said, giving her a stern look. "But she does have a point, Kate. How do you intend to pay for this horse?"

I had to think fast. I had to come up with a plan, or a deal, or something. I looked at Dark Ryder, at the mocking face of Victoria, at the men. Then I stuck one hand in my pocket and felt the resumé I had written this morning. That was it!

"I'll work for you – all summer!" I said. "I'll be a

stable hand, or anything, but I'll do it every day. That's got to be worth a couple thousand dollars."

Doc Vickers smiled. "Sounds like a fair deal to me, Jed. A second ago you were going to put this horse down, and now Kate is offering you a deal that gets the horse out of here for good. Shake hands and make it a deal; we can do the paperwork later."

"Do it, Daddy," Victoria said. "I hate that horse. I never want to see it again."

"Is it a deal, Mr. Peterson?" I asked, putting out my hand.

"Deal," he said, shaking mine. "That damn horse is your problem now, Kate." Then Mr. Peterson turned to his daughter. "Don't worry, honey, we'll get you a better horse. We'll get you one that you'll win lots of ribbons with," he said as he put his arm around her.

Pat, Dr. Vickers and I just watched as the two Petersons walked away to the house.

"Well, looks like you got the deal of the century, kid," Doc Vickers said with a wink. "That was probably the stupidest deal Jed Peterson ever made in his life. But the rest is all up to you."

CHAPTER 5

Telling Gramps

Maybe getting Dark Ryder was a great deal, but as soon as it was done, I got scared. There must have been something about the look on my face that gave a clue to Pat.

"Hey, what's the problem, Kate? You just got a ten-thousand-dollar horse for a summer's worth of work. Even better, you get to have me as your boss."

"Yeah, but, you see ..." and then I explained my great idea to make money for Gramps.

"So listen," Pat replied, "I've got an idea for you. I'll help you work with Dark Ryder through the summer, then you take him to the Royal Winter Fair. If you win all three classes in the junior jumper division, you'll get a couple thousand bucks, for sure."

Could we do it? I wondered. I looked at Dark Ryder and he nudged me with his nose, maybe in answer to my question.

"Now you better go get a stall ready in your barn.

Dark Ryder needs a nice place to stay this summer and Major Mack's going to have a new friend. I'll bring Dark Ryder over when I finish work."

"That gives me time to tell Gramps ..." I said with a lump in my throat. Already I knew that wouldn't be easy.

My gramps was driving our tractor through the field between our house and Mr. Peterson stables. When he saw me coming towards him, he stopped the tractor and turned off the engine.

"What's up, Kate?" he asked when I got up beside him in the cab. "Must be important for you to leave what's-his-name back there."

I took a deep breath and tried to put on my best serious face. "Gramps, there's something important that I need to tell you," I began.

"By the look on your face, you just won a million-dollar lottery," he joked.

So much for my serious face, I thought to myself. "Well, you're almost right ..." I started. "I just bought Victoria's horse, Dark Ryder."

"You what?!" I didn't know if my gramps was shocked or angry or just surprised, but I knew I had to start explaining fast – before he had a chance to cut me off.

"Mr. Peterson didn't want Dark Ryder anymore 'cause Victoria had a fall when she was riding him. He was going to have Dark Ryder put down, but that was too awful so I said I'd buy him. But we don't have any money so I'm going to work all summer to pay for him." All these words came out at a million miles an hour.

"Can I get that again, a little slower?" Gramps asked.

So I told him again, step by step, just what had happened. When I was done, Gramps just sat there in the cab of the tractor, shaking his head.

"Well, I wish I knew how we're going to pay for Dark Ryder's hay and oats. I'm about to lose my shirt on this farm and you bring home another mouth to feed."

"Well, I, uh …" If the farm were in trouble before, I'd just made everything a little bit worse. "I'm sorry, Gramps, but I promise Dark Ryder will earn his keep – and even more!" I said.

"How's he going to do that?" Gramps asked.

The way he said it, I knew he didn't believe me.

"Pat promised to give me lessons on Dark Ryder and he thinks we could maybe win the junior jumpers at the Royal Winter Fair."

"Is that so?" My gramps was starting to look at least a little more interested. "There's a lot of prize money, isn't there?"

"If we get that prize money, you won't have to sell the farm and I can keep Dark Ryder!"

My gramps took off his hat, scratched his head and thought about my idea. He sat there for a long time saying nothing. Around us, I could hear the sound of wind blowing over the field and the buzz of insects in the summer sun.

Then Gramps gave me the decision. "Okay, Kate. I'll give your new horse a chance, but if he doesn't win that money, he's gone. Actually, if he doesn't win at the fair, we'll all be out of here. It's as simple as that."

CHAPTER 6

Competition

The rest of the afternoon I spent in our barn, getting a stall ready for Dark Ryder. Major Mack knew something was up. He kept snorting and stomping while I scrubbed out buckets and put fresh straw in the stall next to his. I'd always thought horses were smart animals and I was pretty sure Major Mack knew he was getting a new friend.

When I had finally finished getting Dark Ryder's stall ready, I gave Major Mack his dinner.

Then I headed up to the house to have my own. My gramps still seemed a little worried about the new horse, but he listened while I told him how Victoria had fallen from Dark Ryder.

"You just be careful – a horse with that much power has to be respected. If not, you'll end up in the dirt just like little Miss Stuck-up," my gramps said.

"We'll be just fine," I said, so sure of myself. "You just have to know how far and how fast to take a horse."

"You got all that figured out with your years and years of experience, eh?" he laughed.

Just then I heard nickering coming from our barn. It was Major Mack. And then I heard another neigh – deep and loud. I knew it was Dark Ryder!

I gulped down my last mouthfuls of food and ran out the door.

I could see Pat leading the big black horse through the field. Dark Ryder was prancing around and snorting, almost pulling Pat off his feet.

"Watch out, Kate," Pat said as I approached. "This guy's a little wild from all the excitement. If

he's like this now, I think you'll have your hands full tomorrow!"

Just as Pat said that, Dark Ryder lunged. He pulled Pat along with him, almost yanking the reins right from his hands.

"Whoa, there, big guy," I said.

Dark Ryder was lathered in sweat and his nostrils were flaring. He looked a lot more frightening than the beautiful horse I had bought that afternoon.

"I'm sure he'll get over this," Pat told me. "He's

just excited 'cause he can hear Major Mack calling him."

"I hope so," I said as I watched Dark Ryder drag Pat all the way to my barn. Back at the house, I could see my gramps standing in the doorway. He must have thought that I had bought myself a wild horse.

"Kate, you better go help Pat open that barn door," Gramps shouted from the house.

Pat was trying to open the barn door while dodging Dark Ryder's hooves. If he didn't watch out, he'd get a hoof in his head and I'd have a wild horse running off.

Stay cool, I told myself. I walked slowly towards the barn so I wouldn't scare the nervous horse, then spoke in a quiet voice, "Whoa, Dark Ryder, easy." I kept whispering the same soft words, then I walked up beside him and slid the barn door open.

Dark Ryder stopped jumping around and just stood there. He was still snorting, but he was looking right at me. I was afraid at first, but I knew I should never show fear to a horse. Instead, I reached out my hand and patted his neck. Dark Ryder seemed to relax right away.

"You sure have a way with this guy," Pat said. He was still holding onto Dark Ryder's rope, but the horse wasn't fighting him now.

"Maybe he knows I'm the one who saved him," I said, reaching up to scratch Dark Ryder's ear.

Inside the barn, Major Mack was pacing up and down in his stall as if he knew something was up. I took the rope from Pat and led my new horse into the barn. It was time for these two horses to meet each other.

At first, both horses were quiet. There seemed to be some mix of pride and fear and question as they looked at each other. Then the two horses sniffed each other, neighed and nickered, and seemed to relax.

"Well how do you do?" laughed Pat. "Major Mack, meet the wildest horse I've ever had the unpleasure of meeting, Dark Ryder."

I led Dark Ryder into the stall beside Major Mack and gave him some hay. The two horses were feeding together now, and they seemed at peace with each other.

Pat walked beside me and looked in at Dark

Ryder. "I don't know what you did to calm him down, Kate, but that sure was amazing," he said.

Then we heard my gramps voice from outside. "Is it safe for an old coot like me to come in there?"

"Of course it is, Gramps," I called out to him. "Dark Ryder isn't that wild."

My gramps walked through the door and came over to the stall to join us. He peered through the bars at Dark Ryder. "Well he sure is a beauty, Kate, but I don't know about his temper. I don't know if I want my little girl –"

"Gramps, I'm not a little girl anymore," I snapped at him. "And I know this horse. Dark Ryder might be a little nervous after all that's happened, but he's not mean."

"Okay, okay, I don't need your temper, too, Kate," Gramps replied. "But the minute this horse hurts you, I'll send him to the glue factory myself!" This time he wasn't joking. "And don't forget our deal, Kate: if you and what's-his-name don't win that money at the Royal Winter Fair, Dark Ryder has got to go." My gramps gave one last look at all of us and left the barn.

I looked over at Dark Ryder and then turned to Pat. It was time to ask the serious question. "Pat – do you think Dark Ryder and I really have a chance?"

Pat nodded and smiled at me. "Of course you do. But you'll have to work hard to make sure Dark Ryder gets over that nervous streak of his."

"Yeah, I know," I sighed.

"And you're going to have some competition," he told me quietly. "Mr. Peterson just bought Victoria a new horse. I haven't seen him yet, but I hear he cost a fortune."

CHAPTER 7

Lessons and a Challenge

It wasn't until the following week that I had my first real lesson with Dark Ryder.

I had been working every day at Mr. Peterson's farm with Pat. Every morning I would wake up at six o'clock and walk over to start my day. In the mornings, we had to feed all of the horses and clean their stalls. By noon, we would finish all that work. Then came my favourite part of the day. Pat had to ride all of Mr. Peterson's young horses, and there were six of them. While Pat was riding, I would get the next horse ready for him. It almost seemed like a factory. I would put the saddle on, and Pat would ride. When he was done, he would hand me the hot horse and take the next one. It was also my job to cool down each horse after Pat rode it.

So after all of this work, I was glad when Pat told me to get Dark Ryder ready for a lesson. I had been doing a little bit of practising at home, but I hadn't tried any jumps with Dark Ryder yet. It was time to get serious – we only had four months to get ready.

When I got out to the ring with my helmet, I saw there was somebody else standing beside Pat, somebody I had seen before. He was an old man, with deep creases in his skin and bushy eyebrows.

"Well, Kate, I got us some help today. I guess you remember Bart Myers."

"Heard about you and this here wild horse, Kate," Mr. Myers said. "Thought you could use a hand."

"Bart's trained a lot of great riders," Pat said. "I figured he could give you some real lessons."

"Well, uh, thanks, Mr. Myers," I said. I really was grateful, I guess, but nervous, too. Now there'd be two men watching me on my new horse.

"Just relax and be natural," Pat told me as we got Dark Ryder ready. "Dark Ryder is smart and knows what he's doing. He just needs a rider with a bit of confidence."

I just kept quiet and nodded. I was too nervous to talk. Confidence would be a great thing – if I had any!

When I got to the ring, Pat gave me a boost onto Dark Ryder's back. I gathered together my reins and started to walk him around the ring. I let him get a good look at all the jumps.

"Well, Kate, you're looking pretty good up there," said Pat from the fence.

"Straighten your back," shouted old Mr. Myers.

I sat tall, just like he said. Then I saw Mr. Peterson come around the corner of the barn and walk past the ring. Out of the corner of my eye, I could tell that he was looking very closely at me and Dark Ryder. But he said nothing, just kept on walking.

"Okay, Kate, time to take Dark Ryder out on a test drive," Pat said. "Try that small jump over there."

"Do you think I'm ready yet?" I asked.

"If Victoria can put this horse over a small fence, you certainly can," said Pat. "Just pay attention to what you're doing and Dark Ryder will do the rest."

"I hope so," I said.

Mr. Myers spoke up, "Before you jump him, Kate, you have to work at relaxing the horse. He has to trust you. Every time you ask Dark Ryder to do something, ask him gently. You're not talking to a horse – you're talking to a baby, got it?"

"Got it," I said. I bent low and whispered to Dark Ryder to trot. Then I squeezed my legs gently against his sides. Immediately, Dark Ryder's ears pricked forward and he started a quick trot. "That's right, Kate," said Mr. Myers, "if you treat him nicely, he'll do whatever you want. Just remember that you guys are a team and you have to work together."

Mr. Myers was right. Dark Ryder and I *are* a team. We're a team that has to beat Victoria and win my gramps that prize money.

We raced forward towards the one small jump in the training ring.

You can do this, I thought to myself.

"You can do this," I whispered to Dark Ryder.

And he did. We cleared that jump so easily that I hardly felt the rise and fall. Then we were racing around the ring, getting ready to do it again. We were on our way when Dark Ryder suddenly leapt to one side. The sudden jerk almost made me fall, but I grabbed his mane and held on.

When I looked up, I saw what had frightened him. Victoria had galloped up to the fence on a big, beautiful grey horse. She just sat there, staring from across the fence at us.

"Victoria, your lesson isn't for another half-hour," said Pat. By the sound of his voice I could tell he was getting mad.

"I just thought I'd watch Kate ride. Daddy says I might learn something – from a *farm* girl." Her voice was full of sarcasm.

Mr. Myers wasn't happy about all this. I don't think he liked Victoria – not at all. "Well you can watch, little girl. But don't you gallop up here like that again."

"Hey, old man, let me remind you that this is *my* farm," she snapped back.

"And I'll remind you that I taught your daddy to ride – and he never once sassed me back. You just watch yourself, girl."

While the two of them were arguing, I looked at Victoria's new horse. I could tell he had cost a lot of money because he had a brand on his hip – the kind of brand that they gave the best horses in Europe. Mr. Peterson must have flown this horse from the other side of the world for his spoiled daughter. I could see how strong and smart the horse was, just by looking. How could a horse like Dark Ryder compete against a horse like that?

Mr. Myers' voice broke into my thoughts. "Okay, Kate, you think you're ready to try the real jumps?" he asked, focusing his attention back to me.

"Uh, I guess," I was suddenly very nervous. Not only would I be doing this in front of Pat and Mr. Myers, but now Victoria was here to watch. I knew she wanted me to make a fool of myself.

Pat looked around the ring at all the jumps that

were set up. Most of them were still set at their maximum height, like they were when Victoria had fallen from Dark Ryder. Mr. Myers lifted his arm and pointed at one of the bigger jumps. It was the same jump that Victoria had tried and fallen off Dark Ryder!

I gulped. The only jumps I had ever done were half that big. "I … I don't think that I'm ready –"

"Kate, do you want to show at the Royal Winter Fair?" Mr. Myers asked me.

"Yes, but –"

"Then you better get used to jumps like that because they're all that big," he said.

So I gathered Dark Ryder's reins into my hands and took a deep breath. I took one look around at Pat, Mr. Myers and Victoria and then turned all my attention to Dark Ryder.

I asked him to trot and then squeezed my legs again to get him to go faster and into a canter. "Okay boy, let's show Victoria that we can do this," I whispered to Dark Ryder. Then we came around the corner and started towards the jump.

I stared right at the jump. It looked like a giant wall right in front of us. Dark Ryder only had five more strides before he had to clear it. I leaned a bit forward and wrapped my fingers around his mane. *You can do this*, I said to myself, or maybe I said it out loud. But I knew Dark Ryder could do this jump, I just had to trust him – and stay on!

Four, three, two, one – I felt Dark Ryder's front legs leave the ground. Just like that we were flying through the air. The loud thump of our landing brought me back to reality. I sat back in the saddle and pulled on the reins to get Dark Ryder to stop.

Pat was clapping and shouting, "Nice job, kid!" Mr. Myers didn't say anything, but he looked pleased. Only Victoria was silent. I had cleared the jump that she hadn't. And that made her angry.

"That's enough for today, Kate. You did a great job!" Pat called to me. "It's time for Victoria's lesson."

Pat came up and held Dark Ryder as I dismounted. Then he took the reins and started leading Dark Ryder back to the barn.

I followed behind, in shock at what I had just done. It was Victoria who broke my daydream. She rode up beside me on her big grey horse.

"So you must think you're something now," she said with a sneer. "Just don't get your hopes up, Kate. One jump doesn't mean you can do a whole course."

"I know that," I said, glaring back at her.

"Besides, Dark Ryder doesn't stand a chance against King Jack," she said, patting the big grey horse.

"So your new horse's name is King Jack?" I asked, trying to be polite.

"Yes," she replied. "He's won every show he's ever been in, and I don't plan on breaking the streak. Face it, Kate, you haven't got a hope at the Royal Winter Fair."

"At least I could do that jump without falling off," I shot back.

"At least I don't have to settle for someone else's hand-me-down horse," replied Victoria. With that, she rode into the ring to get ready for her lesson.

First Major Mack was a donkey, and now she

was calling Dark Ryder a hand-me-down! I gritted my teeth and gave Victoria one last look. I had to win at the Royal Winter Fair, not just for the money, but to prove Victoria wrong.

CHAPTER 8

Doubts

When I got to the barn, Pat already had Dark Ryder unsaddled.

"Why do you look so mad?" he asked when he saw me. "You should be grinning, the way you took that jump with Dark Ryder."

"Yeah," I muttered, not really in a mood to be cheered up.

"Okay, what did the Princess say when you walked by?" Pat asked.

"She called Dark Ryder a hand-me-down, and told me we didn't have a hope at the Royal Winter Fair."

Pat shook his head and smiled. "Don't worry, she's just scared that she'll get beat. Even with that expensive horse of hers, I think you can win the prizes," Pat said.

"Thanks," I replied, still angry at Victoria.

"Speaking of hand-me-downs, I saw a nice girl's show jacket and boots over in the tack room," Pat said, and then he winked at me.

"Whose are they?" I asked, not quite getting it.

"Mr. Myers has a daughter who doesn't ride much anymore. These are her old show clothes. He figured you wouldn't have any, so he wants you to wear them at the horse show," Pat said.

"Really?" I was surprised.

"Yeah, his daughter moved into the city and isn't too interested in horses these days ... too busy making money in the stock market," said Pat. "I guess Mr. Myers figures you'll put those clothes to better use than she ever will."

That made me break into a grin. Old Mr. Myers

must believe that I actually stood a chance if he was thinking about what I would wear at the show. I left Pat at the stable and went into the tack room to look at the jacket and boots.

The jacket was navy blue and cut in a style that was a little out of date, but I could tell by looking that it had been expensive. The boots were scuffed, but I knew a little polish would get them to shine like brand new. I had just put on the jacket when I heard someone walk in the room behind me.

"Looks like it fits okay," old Mr. Myers said.

"Pat told me you wanted me to wear these things at the show," I said.

"Yeah, they always brought my daughter good luck, so maybe they'll do the same with you," he said, looking a little sad.

"Are you sure about this, Mr. Myers?" I asked.

"Yeah, I'm sure," he said, waiting for a second. "It's just that …well, the way you were riding today, you reminded me of my own kid. She never took the top prizes at the fair," he sighed, "but I think you just might."

I didn't know what to say. I loved the jacket and

boots, and I was glad that Mr. Myers thought I might win. But all this was just more pressure to win at the Royal Winter Fair.

"Thanks, Mr. Myers, I won't let you down," I heard myself say, but I didn't really believe my own words as they came out.

That night at dinner I thought about how all these people were depending on me. Dark Ryder wouldn't have a home if we didn't win, and neither would me or my gramps. And then there was Mr. Myers …

"Kate?" Gramps broke into my train of thought.

"Yeah, Gramps?" I replied.

"Are you sure this plan with Dark Ryder is going to work? I mean, he's worth a pretty penny, even with that temper of his – "

"What are you talking about?" I cut in.

"Well, I was thinking…. The bank called today and they're putting a bit of pressure on me, kind of leaning pretty hard on that loan I took out. So I thought about Dark Ryder and what he might be worth. You know, Kate, a little cash in the pocket beats a roll of the dice at the fair."

"What?!" I shouted, pushing myself away from the table. "I can't believe you could even think of selling my horse," I yelled. "I mean, you'd never sell Major Mack no matter how much trouble you were in. Why should I have to sell *my* horse?"

"I *would* sell Major Mack if I could find

somebody who'd buy him," Gramps snapped back. It was the first time I'd heard him talk like this.

"But Dark Ryder's going to win us that prize money," I replied.

"And what if he doesn't?" my gramps asked.

"He will," I said, my voice near tears. "I just know he will."

Later that night, I heard Gramps come up the stairs. I heard him get ready for bed, but I didn't open my door to say good night. When I heard Gramps start snoring, I crept out of my room and down the stairs.

In the living room, I saw a picture of my parents and me, way back before the accident. We were all smiling at the camera, so sure that all our lives would turn out all right. Only a year after that, they were both dead in a car crash and I was coming out of the hospital, not badly hurt but half dead inside. We'd had big hopes back then, and they had come to nothing. *Please, not again*, I prayed. *This time just give me a chance*. There were tears in my eyes as I walked out to the barn.

Dark Ryder made a shuffling sound with his

hoofs when I opened the barn door. I walked to his stall and let myself in. Dark Ryder sniffed me and then put his head on my shoulder while I hugged him around the neck.

"You can do it," I whispered to him – or myself. *You can do it!*

CHAPTER 9

Off to the Fair

I worked at Mr. Peterson's farm for the rest of the summer, buying my horse, week after week. A couple of times Mr. Peterson tried to talk me out of the deal, but I held him to it. Now Dark Ryder was signed over to me, and the pressure was really on.

Just before school began, I ran into Victoria after a lesson. "Only two months until the Royal Winter Fair," she said to me. "Think you're going to be ready?"

"We're ready right now," I shot back.

"So well spoken, *farm girl*," she said. Then she turned and walked away from me.

"Of course you're ready," Pat told me. "The Princess is just being a snot. Don't let her get to you."

I rolled my eyes and tried to act like it was no big deal. For more than two months, I had spent every weekend working at Mr. Myers' farm. That got me two free lessons a week. On the days that I didn't have lessons, Pat would let me practice at the Peterson farm. When I knocked a fence down with

Dark Ryder, Pat would set it back up again. When Dark Ryder was acting nervous, Pat would talk to him gently and calm him down.

Almost before we knew it, it was the week of the Royal Winter Fair. Were we ready? Pat said he had confidence in me, and Mr. Myers said I was as good as I was going to get. But was that good enough?

Mr. Myers offered to take Dark Ryder to the fair with his horse trailer, since my gramps had sold his long ago. Mr. Myers said we had to go in early so Dark Ryder he could get used to the new stable. My gramps had to stay home and look after the farm, but he promised he'd drive up to watch me ride the next day.

I could hear Dark Ryder stomping in the horse trailer as we pulled into the fair grounds. I could tell that the noise of the big city was making him nervous. As soon as we stopped, I ran back to the trailer to pat him and calm him down.

"Better let me take him into the stable, Kate," Mr. Myers said as he came up behind me. "This is a busy place and Dark Ryder's going to feel if you're nervous. And that's going to make *him* nervous, so let this old guy do it."

I nodded and stepped back so Mr. Myers could take Dark Ryder out of the trailer. Pat let down the trailer ramp and Mr. Myers slowly backed Dark Ryder out. As soon as Dark Ryder's feet hit the ground, he let out a big neigh.

"He's just telling all the other horses that he's going to kick butt," Pat said to me.

"Yeah, well, I hope so," I replied. I tried to sound a little more confident than I really felt.

Mr. Myers lead Dark Ryder into the arena and stable area where he would be staying overnight. We settled Dark Ryder into his stall and gave him his dinner for the night. Then Pat and I decided to check out the show ring where I would be riding.

"Do you want to come with us?" Pat asked Mr. Myers.

"I've seen that ring a million times, son," said Mr. Myers. "I'm just going to stay here and take a nap with this horse of yours."

So Pat and I walked by ourselves over to the big arena where the show was going to take place.

70

There were about ten horses and riders practising when we got there. Pat and I sat down on the bleachers and watched the horses and riders go around and attempt the jumps. I could see that every horse there was just as good as Dark Ryder – if not better. I felt like my heart was sinking into my stomach.

"Hey, you," Pat said, nudging me with his shoulder.

"Hey, yourself," I replied.

"You're not sounding too cheerful, Kate," Pat said to me.

"Those horses look too good," I told him. "You know what's at stake. If we don't win tomorrow, I'm going to lose Dark Ryder and my gramps is going to lose his farm."

"You've got to think positive. We've been practising for three months now – and you're just as good as these people riding right now," Pat said as he pointed to the ring. "Probably even better …" and with that he grabbed my hand and gave it a squeeze.

I squeezed his hand back, and then we just kept

on holding hands. I don't know if it was romantic, or just friendly, or what. But it felt good. And my heart, scared as it was, began beating a little faster.

CHAPTER 10

Round One

Even though I fall asleep easily, I could hardly sleep that night. When the first light of dawn broke, I was already up and dressed. While Mr. Myers and Pat slept, I gave Dark Ryder his grain and hay and changed his water. Then I got to work polishing the boots Mr. Myers had loaned me. I wanted them to shine when I got into the ring.

I had just finished the first boot and was working on the second when Pat and Mr. Myers both came

in. "Looks like someone's a little antsy this morning," said Mr. Myers when he saw me. I just gave him a nervous smile, then turned my eyes to Pat.

But Pat didn't really look at me at all. He just grabbed some brushes and started grooming Dark Ryder. By nine, Pat had brushed Dark Ryder so much that his coat was glistening. I had polished my boots so shiny that I could see my reflection in them. Neither of us talked about holding hands the night before. All three of us waited awkwardly for the announcer to call the riders.

At 10:30, the announcer's voice came over the loud speaker. He said it was our turn to walk around the ring and look at the course of jumps.

"Do you want me to walk the course with you?" Mr. Myers asked.

I nodded, still not able to speak. There was a lump in my stomach, as if I'd swallowed a baseball for breakfast.

When the two of us got up to leave, I looked at Pat. "You're coming too, aren't you?" I asked him.

"If you want me to," he replied.

"Of course I do," I said, smiling at him. "You're ... important," I said, after looking for the word.

Pat smiled shyly at me, but he got the message. Then the three of us walked to the ring. Most of the riders were already out walking the course when we got there. "Now, when you first get in, you're going to want to let Dark Ryder take a good look around. Don't push him. You don't want a nervous horse on your hands, not today," Mr. Myers lectured me.

I was trying my best to listen, when I heard some alughter behind me. It was Victoria talking to one of her friends. "So how's hand-me-down girl?" she asked as she looked at what I was wearing.

I just ignored her and kept listening to Mr. Myers. "… and over here there's a sharp turn, so make sure you – "

"Oooohhh, *farm girl* thinks she's too good to talk to me," I could hear Victoria saying. "But she won't think she's so hot when I beat her and she loses Dark Ryder."

I stopped listening to Mr. Myers. How did Victoria know my gramps was going to sell Dark Ryder if I didn't win?

Pat must have seen the look on my face. He squeezed my hand again and said, "Don't worry, she's just trying to get to you."

I swallowed hard and tried to keep myself from getting angry. But the baseball in my gut was feeling bigger and bigger.

We finished walking around the course. All the

jumps were big, but I knew Dark Ryder would have no problem handling them. So long as I could keep Dark Ryder calm and easy, we'd be okay.

I was the second-last person to ride in my group, so I had lots of time to see the competition. When everyone was done walking the course, we waited by the ring to watch the first few riders.

The first horse that stepped into the ring was a big chestnut with a white stripe down his face. His rider looked like a guy about Pat's age. They did a circle and then headed towards the first jump. I could tell that that the big chestnut was a hyper horse by the way the guy was pulling on his reins. They did the first two jumps quickly, but by the third jump, the horse seemed to have taken control. The big chestnut hit the top rail with his back legs – a knockdown! The gate was opened and the chestnut horse left the ring, sweating and breathing hard.

We watched another two riders attempt the course, but neither of them had a clear round. They missed one or another of the jumps, or touched one of the rails. The course might not have looked hard, but the other riders were having a tough time with it.

I saw my gramps just as we were about to leave and get Dark Ryder ready.

"I told you I'd get here," he said as he walked up to us.

"Well, you're just in time. I'm about to go get Dark Ryder ready," I said. Mr. Myers and Pat had already started walking towards the stables, and I wanted to catch up with them.

As I turned to leave, I heard my gramp's voice. "Do your best, Kate, that's all that counts."

"I know, Gramps, I know ..." I said as the tight ball in my gut seemed to twist and turn.

Over at the stable, Pat and Mr. Myers already had Dark Ryder's saddle on his back. I quickly put on my jacket, boots and helmet. "You look like a pro," said Pat when he saw me in my outfit.

If only I felt like one, I thought to myself.

Mr. Myers led Dark Ryder into the warm-up ring, with me following behind. Then he gave me a boost onto Dark Ryder's back.

"Just ride him around here a few times and take

one or two practice jumps," he said. "He's going to be nervous, so keep talking to him." Mr. Myers let go of Dark Ryder's reins and handed them to me. "Oh, and good luck, kid."

Who's going to calm me down? I thought to myself. At the other end of the warm-up ring, I could see Victoria with her new horse, King Jack.

I looked down at Dark Ryder. He was snorting. I could sense he was nervous, but somehow I think he knew this show was important.

Just like Mr. Myers had told me, I asked Dark Ryder gently to trot. As soon as I touched my legs to his side, he shot forward. "Whoa, boy," I said as I pulled on the reins to tell him to slow down a bit. "Easy, easy, easy does it," I kept saying as we trotted around the ring.

Dark Ryder seemed to be settling down, when a grey shape cut quickly in front of us. My horse jerked back and almost reared up from sheer fright.

"Oops, didn't see you there," came the voice. It was Victoria. She had cut both of us off, and now Dark Ryder snorting and jumping away from every noise in the ring.

"Whoa …" I said, trying to ignore Victoria. I knew I had to calm down Dark Ryder. He couldn't be afraid when we stepped into that ring, otherwise we'd never make it all around the course. So I whispered to him, "We can do this, boy, we can do it." And I whispered the same to myself, *We can do this, we can do this – if we're not afraid.*

There wasn't much time before we would be called into the show ring, so I had to take a practice jump soon. When Dark Ryder calmed down a bit, I pointed him to the jump in the centre of the warm-up ring and took a deep breath. "Okay, boy, let's go," I said. We headed toward the jump, slowly at first, then faster and faster. Dark Ryder pricked his ears and cantered towards the jump full force. He made a powerful leap that easily cleared the rail. When we landed, I knew we were both ready. *We can do this,* I repeated to myself.

I walked Dark Ryder over to where Pat and Mr. Myers were standing. Only five minutes until I would be in the ring.

"Not one rider has finished the course without a fault," said Pat. "It looks pretty tough out there."

"Thanks, Pat, that's all I need to hear," I said, making a face at him.

"Hey, if I was worried about you, I wouldn't say anything."

"Hey, yourself," I said back. "We're ready."

Then I heard my number called. I looked at Pat and Mr. Myers, then picked up my reins and trotted Dark Ryder right into the ring.

I took a look at the crowd – a thousand faces looked back at me. My heart started racing, but then I got control of myself. *Stay calm, Kate*, I told myself. I bent down and whispered to my horse, "Okay, guy, don't knock any jumps down and we'll do fine."

I heard the signal bell to start. Carefully I circled Dark Ryder and pointed him towards the first fence. From his snorting I could tell he was afraid, but he kept going. "We can do this," I told him. And we did – the first jump was a breeze.

I looked to the second jump and forgot about how much my gramps needed the prize money and how I might lose Dark Ryder. I just kept my mind on the course and Dark Ryder. "We can do

this one, too," I said to him – or maybe to myself.

As we cleared each jump, I started to realize we might just win. Dark Ryder was still in control, still taking each jump as it came. Finally, we were headed towards the final jump.

"We can really do this, really, *really*," I said to Dark Ryder. Maybe he heard me, or maybe he knew we were close to the end. I'll never know. I felt Dark Ryder pick up speed for the last jump, daring himself to go faster and faster. He pricked his ears forward and then took a giant leap.

As we came down, I could hear the crowd cheering. We had done it – all twelve jumps with no faults. I hugged Dark Ryder and gave a thumbs-up to my gramps, who was now standing with Mr. Myers and Pat. There was only one rider and horse pair left. If they didn't go clear, I had won the class!

As I left the show ring, I could see who my only competition was. A grey horse and his blonde rider – Victoria.

"That was awesome, Kate," Pat said as soon as he saw me. "You guys looked so focused out there. I don't think anything could have broken your concentration."

But I wasn't listening to him. I wanted to see how Victoria would ride the course. The judge rang the bell and Victoria and King Jack started the course.

As I watched them go around, I could see why Mr. Myers had bought King Jack. He took the jumps like they were stepping stones. Victoria didn't even need to be riding. King Jack just knew automatically what to do. I felt my heart sink as I watched Victoria and King Jack clear the last jump. They had gone clear as well. Now there would be a jumpoff between me and my worst enemy!

CHAPTER 11

It's Not Over Yet

"Looks like it's not over yet," said Mr. Myers after a long pause.

"Well, dang it," my gramps added.

I saw Victoria ride over to her father, grinning. Mr. Peterson was patting King Jack and looked just as happy as his daughter.

The announcer came on the speakers. "There is a tie between Victoria Peterson and Kate Hanson. The course will be shortened to six jumps and there will be a jumpoff round. Whoever completes the course in the fastest time with the least number of faults will win. Kate Hanson will go first."

"Don't worry about how fast you go," said Mr. Myers as we walked back to the stables and untied Dark Ryder. I had Pat boost me up onto Dark Ryder's back while I listened to Mr. Myers' advice. "If you start pushing Dark Ryder too hard, he might make a mistake. Just ride how you always do and you'll be fine."

"Stay cool, Kate," Pat added.

"Okay," I said, my stomach still in knots. "But if King Jack and Victoria do the jumpoff like they just did that course, we're going to be in trouble."

Mr. Myers and my gramps both wished me good luck. Pat gave me another thumbs-up as I rode into the ring again. Even though I knew Mr. Myers was right about not pushing Dark Ryder to go too fast, I knew I had to. If I was going to beat Victoria, it would have to be with speed.

I steered Dark Ryder towards the first jump, I squeezed his sides a little bit harder than I usually would. But Dark Ryder didn't panic. He picked up the pace and jumped the first fence clean as could be. I rode to each fence like that, pushing Dark Ryder to go faster each time. When we reached the sixth jump, we were going faster that I'd ever been on a horse. The ground, the crowd, the fences were all a blur. It was all I could do to hang on as Dark Ryder went up.

And came down – perfectly! I looked up at my time flashing across the screen. Forty-two seconds! I knew Victoria would have to ride as fast as she possibly could to beat that.

I walked Dark Ryder out of the show ring as Mr. Myers, Pat and my gramps all came to congratulate me. Then we turned our attention back to the ring. Like Mr. Myers had said, it wasn't over yet. Victoria trotted King Jack into the centre of the ring and smiled at the crowd.

"What a show-off," I muttered to myself.

"I bet the Princess is sweating a little," said Pat.

The bell rang and once again Victoria started her ride. This time she gave King Jack a big crack with her whip so he would go faster than ever. King Jack immediately took off, flying over each fence.

At the speed Victoria was going, I knew she was going to beat me. Two, three, four, five fences without one problem. I felt Pat reach down and grab my hand.

Only one more fence and I could see Victoria's time was going to beat mine. Then, at the last minute, Victoria looked away from the jump. She stared straight at me, as if to rub in my face the fact that she had won.

Victoria wasn't paying full attention when King Jack took his final leap. And that was a big mistake. The jump caught her off balance, and just as she had with Dark Ryder, she fell. This time, she landed squarely on her butt.

There was a cry from the audience, and then the announcer summed it all up. "The Junior Amateur Jumper winner is Kate Hanson."

"You did it, Katie," my grandfather cried. "You and that darned horse did it!" My gramps was so excited he put his arms around me and hugged me so hard I couldn't breathe. Mr. Myers and Pat were cheering and even Dark Ryder let out a neigh.

In the ring, Victoria stood up and was cleaning the dirt off of her pants. Mr. Peterson had caught

King Jack and was helping his daughter to the exit gate.

I led Dark Ryder into the centre of the show ring, where the judge gave me a trophy and the prize money. Mr. Myers and my gramps stood by while a photographer took a picture of Dark Ryder and me.

Then I saw Pat coming towards me with a giant bouquet of flowers. "I got these for you last night," he said, turning a little red. "No matter whether you won or lost, I thought you still deserved them."

"Thanks, Pat," I said, taking the flowers from him.

Then he leaned in and kissed me – I couldn't believe it. I mean, it wasn't a great big romantic kiss, but it was a real kiss. My first kiss ever! Pat and

I were still looking at each other, feeling kind of awkward, when I heard Mr. Peterson's voice.

"Okay, Kate, you win. I'll buy that stupid horse back from you. How much do you want?"

He had his cheque book out and was waving it in front of our faces. For a second, I didn't know what to do or what to say. We had won, we had the prize money, and now we could get ten or twenty thousand more.

But before I could say a word, my gramps jumped in ahead of me. "Dark Ryder isn't for sale," Gramps said flatly. "He's got a lot of good shows ahead of him – and Kate's going to take him to all of them."

Our Plane Is Down
by DOUG PATON

A small plane goes down in the bush, hours from anywhere. The radio is broken, the pilot is out cold. There's only a little water and even less food. Can Cal make it through the woods to save his sister, the pilot and himself?

Against All Odds
by PAUL KROPP

Nothing ever came easy for Jeff. He had a tough time at school and hung around with all the wrong kids in the neighborhood. But when he and his brother are drowning in a storm sewer, Jeff is the one who never gives up.

Student Narc
by PAUL KROPP

It wasn't Kevin's idea to start working with the cops. But when his best friend dies from an overdose, somebody has to do something. Kevin finally takes on a whole drug gang – and their boss – in a struggle that leaves him scarred for life.

The Kid Is Lost
by PAUL KROPP

It's a babysitter's worst nightmare: a child goes missing! Kurt has to get help and lead the search into a deadly swamp on his ATV. Will he find the lost child in time?

About the Author

Liz Brown has loved horses ever since she was a little girl, long before she went to Ryerson University to study journalism. She was lucky enough to grow up on a horse farm with two ponies, Misty and Frosty. Like Kate in *Dark Ryder*, Liz always wanted to show a horse at the Royal Winter Fair in Toronto. She finally got the chance in 2002, but didn't do quite as well as Kate in the competition. Liz now divides her time between magazine journalism and teaching kids how to ride. *Dark Ryder* is her first novel.

High Interest Publishing – Publishers of H·I·P Books
407 Wellesley Street East • Toronto, Ontario M4X 1H5
www.hip-books.com